The American Girls

1764 **Kaya**, an adventurous Nez Perce girl whose deep love for horses and respect for nature nourish her spirit

1774 **Felicity**, a spunky, spritely colonial girl, full of energy and independence

1824 **Josefina**, a Hispanic girl whose heart and hopes are as big as the New Mexico sky

1854 **Kirsten**, a pioneer girl of strength and spirit who settles on the frontier

1864 **Addy**, a courageous girl determined to be free in the midst of the Civil War

1904 **Samantha**, a bright Victorian beauty, an orphan raised by her wealthy grandmother

1934 **Kit**, a clever, resourceful girl facing the Great Depression with spirit and determination

1944 **Molly**, who schemes and dreams on the home front during World War Two

1944

BRAVE
Emily

BY VALERIE TRIPP

ILLUSTRATIONS NICK BACKES

VIGNETTES RENÉE GRAEF, SUSAN MCALILEY, AND KEITH SKEEN

★ American Girl™

Questions or comments? Call 1-800-845-0005, visit our Web site at
americangirl.com, or write to Customer Service, American Girl,
8400 Fairway Place, Middleton, WI 53562.

Printed in China
06 07 08 09 10 11 12 LEO 12 11 10 9 8 7 6 5 4 3 2 1

All American Girl marks, Emily™, Emily Bennett™,
Molly®, and Molly McIntire® are trademarks of American Girl, LLC.

Flutophone® used under license from Grover Musical Products, Inc., Cleveland, Ohio.

PICTURE CREDITS
The following individuals and organizations have generously given
permission to reprint images contained in "Looking Back":

p. 69—© Hulton-Deutsch Collection/Corbis (three British children awaiting evacuation);
pp. 70–71—Corbis (bombing of London); Imperial War Museum, London (London tube station,
poster [PST:0076], evacuée tag [EPH:003764]); © Bettmann/Corbis (children evacuating London);
pp. 72–73—© Paul Hardy/Corbis (British flag); © Reg Speller/Hulton Archive/Getty Images
(British girls); Imperial War Museum, London (evacuation ship [HU:89284],
tag and telegram [87/23/1]); courtesy Vintage Posters ("Safe" poster);
pp. 74–75—Greater London Photographic Library (garden tea);
Imperial War Museum, London (poster [PST:5873]); private collection (girls reading letter);
© Bettmann/Corbis (Kindertransport arrival, trainside farewell);
pp. 76–77—© Corbis (Japanese Americans being relocated, Japanese American child);
National Archives (baseball game); © Bettmann/Corbis (Eleanor Roosevelt);
Popperfoto (reunion).

Cataloging-in-Publication Data available from the Library of Congress.

TO HELEN NATALIE FRANCES HEUER,
WITH LOVE

TABLE OF CONTENTS

EMILY'S FRIENDS

EMILY'S FRIENDS

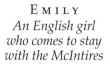

EMILY
*An English girl
who comes to stay
with the McIntires*

MOLLY
*A nine-year-old
who is growing up
on the home front
in America during
World War Two*

SUSAN
*One of Molly's best
friends, a cheerful
dreamer*

LINDA
*One of Molly's best
friends, a practical
schemer*

MRS. MCINTIRE
Molly's mother, who welcomes Emily into the McIntire home

BRAD
Molly's five-year-old brother

MRS. GILFORD
The housekeeper, who rules the roost when Molly's mother is at work

RICKY
Molly's twelve-year-old brother

MISS CAMPBELL
Molly and Emily's teacher, who keeps her third graders on their toes

CHAPTER
ONE

JUST-BEGINNING FRIENDS

Emily Bennett and Molly McIntire were sitting on the floor in the cozy space between the beds in Molly's room. Emily was writing a letter and Molly was doing math homework. When Molly finished, she handed her paper to Emily, who put her letter down, tucked her hair behind her ears, and went to work checking Molly's answers. Molly crossed her fingers and watched anxiously.

At last Emily looked up, her eyes bright. "Jolly good, Molly," she said. "Not one mistake."

"Ya-hoo!" exploded Molly, cheering happily. She jumped up, kicked off her shoes, and began to bounce on her bed. "Hurray! I never could have done it without your help, Emily! Thanks!"

Emily smiled at Molly's exuberance and said, "You're welcome," although she knew that Molly was cheering too loudly to hear her.

"What's all the noise about *now?*" asked Molly's older brother, Ricky, poking his head in the door.

Molly thrust the paper under Ricky's nose. "Look!" she said. "It's the nine times tables, and I got them *all* right."

"Big deal," scoffed Ricky.

"It is to *me*," said Molly. "I've never done it before. Emily showed me how. Tell him, Emily."

Emily hesitated. She didn't have a brother, so she felt rather shy of Ricky, who teased a lot. It seemed unlikely to her that Ricky would be interested in the math that she and Molly were doing. But Ricky was leaning against the door frame, waiting. So Emily gathered her courage and said, "The numerals in the answer always add up to nine."

"And the numeral in the tens column is always one less than the number you're multiplying by nine," Molly said. "Right, Emily?"

"Quite," answered Emily.

Ricky squinted, thinking. Then he shrugged and

said again, "Big deal." But as he left he added, "Your friend Emily is pretty smart for a girl, Molly."

"My friend Emily is pretty smart for *anybody*," crowed Molly, back to bouncing.

Emily glowed. She was pleased that Ricky had called her smart. But she was even more pleased that Molly had called her "my friend."

Emily was staying with Molly's family. She had come by ship from England to America to be safe because London, where she usually lived, was being bombed. Emily's parents were still in London, and Emily had been supposed to stay with her aunt. But Aunt Primrose was in the hospital with pneumonia, so Mrs. McIntire had very kindly taken Emily in until her aunt was better. Molly had been very nice and polite

London's Big Ben

ever since Emily had arrived six days ago, but she'd never actually called Emily her friend before. *If Molly said that I am her friend, then it must be true, mustn't it?* Emily asked herself. *We're friends, or at least just-beginning friends.* Emily certainly hoped so. She thought that Molly was a wonderful girl! She wanted to be Molly's friend very much—very much indeed.

"Come on, Emily," Molly said now. "Mom's home!" She waved her math homework like a flag. "Let's go show her this."

"Right-oh," said Emily. She followed Molly down the stairs into the warm, bright kitchen. All the rooms in the McIntires' house seemed warm and bright to Emily. In England, houses were cold because heating coal was scarce. Rooms were dimly lit and windows were covered with thick blackout curtains at night so that German bombers couldn't see any lights to drop their bombs on.

Mrs. McIntire was sitting at the kitchen table in her Red Cross uniform. Brad, Molly's little brother, and Jill, her older sister, were at the table, too. "Hello, girls," said Mrs. McIntire. "We're having some toast. Would you like to join us?"

Emily said, "Yes, please." She sat next to Brad, who immediately slid half of his toast to her. Emily had noticed that Brad liked to take care of her. Sweetly, he seemed to think that it was his responsibility to see that she was not hungry or unhappy. Of course that was silly, because Brad was only five. But Emily, who hated to be made fun of herself, did not laugh at him. "Thank you, Brad," she said solemnly as she took the toast.

Meanwhile Molly skidded across the kitchen floor in her stocking feet, exclaiming, "Mom! Jill! Emily taught me a way to remember the nine times tables and I got them all right. Look!"

Mrs. McIntire smiled as she looked at Molly's paper. "Very good, olly Molly," she said.

Jill said, "That's an improvement."

"Hey, Emily," Molly asked as she plunked down at the table. "How'd you get to be so good at math?"

Emily blushed at Molly's compliment. "Well," she said thoughtfully, "I like numbers because they are precise. Numbers never lie. In math, your answer is either right or wrong. And the right answer will never change. You can be sure of it."

"Maybe *you* can be sure of your answers," sighed Molly. "But I can't be sure of mine. For instance, I always have to guess at 8 times 7. You've just *absolutely got* to think of a way for me to remember the answer to *that* one, Emily."

"Very well," said Emily earnestly. She was determined not to disappoint Molly.

"Time to get ready for bed," said Mrs. McIntire. "Up you go. Molly and Emily, please take Brad with you and help him brush his teeth. I'll come tuck you in later after Jill and I tidy up the kitchen."

"Okay, Mom," said Molly.

Brad took Emily by the hand. "One, two, three, four," he said, counting each step as he went up the stairs. "See, Emily? I'm good at numbers, too."

"Yes, indeed you are," said Emily.

"Five, six, seven, eight," Brad continued.

Something clicked in Emily's head. "Molly," she said eagerly. "I've thought of a way, just as you told me to."

"A way to what?" asked Molly as they followed Brad down the hall to the bathroom.

"A way to remember 8 times 7," said Emily.

"Gosh!" Molly laughed, handing Brad his toothbrush. "I didn't mean you *really* had to. I was just kidding."

"Oh!" said Emily, embarrassed. Evidently, when Molly had said "absolutely," she hadn't meant *absolutely.* Emily sighed to herself. Even though British and Americans both spoke English, it seemed to Emily that they spoke different kinds of English.

First of all, there were different names for things, like *cookies* for biscuits, *sweater* for jumper, and *sneakers* for plimsolls. Americans pronounced words differently, too. They put an *r* as hard as a growl in the middle of *girl* and at the end of *dear* and *number.* But what Emily found most difficult was the way Americans—or at least Molly and her friends—joked and exaggerated, so that Emily couldn't tell if they meant what they said or not. Indeed, sometimes they meant the exact *opposite* of what they'd said. Emily often felt just as much in a fog in conversations as she'd been on the ship crossing the foggy Atlantic Ocean!

But Molly seemed truly interested when she asked, "What's your idea, Emily? I'd love to know. I need all the help I can get."

"Well," Emily explained, "8 times 7 is 56, so of course that means that 7 times 8 is 56. To remember, start with the answer. Say, '56 equals 7 times 8.' Then think of the numerals and just count: 5, 6, 7, 8."

"Five, six, seven, eight," Brad singsonged, skipping off to his bedroom.

"Hurray!" whooped Molly. " 5, 6—that's 56— equals 7, 8—that's 7 times 8." Emily found herself grabbed up in an impulsive hug as Molly exclaimed, "Thanks, Emily! Hey, you know what? When it comes to math, I can really count on you. Get it?"

Emily's eyes twinkled. Puns were the sort of humor she was used to. "When it comes to math, it all adds up," she said.

"Good one!" Molly laughed. Then she said, "Let's hurry and get into our pajamas so that we  can look at your scrapbook and the pictures of the princesses in it before we go to bed."

"Jolly good!" said Emily. Just the night before, Emily had discovered that Molly liked the two English princesses, Elizabeth and Margaret Rose, as much as she did. Even though the suitcase Emily had brought with her on the ship to America was very small, she had tucked into it her scrapbook with photographs of her family and the princesses. Now she was very glad that she had, because the scrapbook had turned out to be an important part of her just-beginning friendship with Molly.

In a jiffy, the girls were in their pajamas, robes, and slippers. They sat on the floor between the beds again, with the scrapbook across their laps. When Emily opened it, a little tan booklet fell out.

"Is this your ration book?" Molly asked, holding it up.

Emily nodded, not trusting herself to talk. It made her homesick to see the ration book because it made her think of London, and Mum and Dad, and it reminded her how much she missed them.

"Oh, look," said Molly. "Your mom wrote you a note on the back of your ration book. What does the note say?"

Emily knew the note by heart, but she cleared her throat and read, "'Emily, darling girl, Be good. Be tidy. Be obedient. Be honest. And most of all, be polite and grateful. Unrationed love, Mum.'" Emily swallowed hard.

Molly patted Emily's hand kindly. "You miss your parents, don't you?" she asked.

Emily nodded again.

"I'm sure they miss you, too," said Molly. "They must love you very much to part with you and send you here."

That made Emily feel better.

Molly pointed to the note on Emily's ration book.

"You know what, Emily?" she said. "If I went away, I bet my mother would write me the exact same note with the exact same advice in it!"

That made Emily feel better, too.

"We have ration books, too," said Molly as she looked through Emily's. "I guess Mom will get an American one for you. You'll like it, I think. We learned in school that your rationing in England is lots stricter than ours is here. You couldn't have hardly any meat or eggs or milk or fruit."

"Yes," said Emily, "and most of those things are hardly ever in the shops anyway. You can't get them even if you have ration points *and* plenty of money. Meat's so scarce that Mum and the other ladies stand in *queue*—a line, you call it—for hours if word gets out that the butcher has any meat. We grow our own vegetables. We have a garden just like your housekeeper, Mrs. Gilford, has."

"She loves it when you help her in the Victory garden," said Molly.

"Does she?" asked Emily. "I like it, too. It reminds me of home."

"Do me a favor," said Molly. "Promise me that you'll bury all the turnips or ask the Red Cross to

send them to England or something." She slid Emily
a sideways grin. "Just kidding!"

Emily grinned back. She disliked turnips, too.

Molly looked at the pictures in the scrapbook
and sighed. "Don't you just love the princesses'
hair?" she asked. "I wish I had curls like they do."

"I do, too," said Emily. "Or glamorous waves,
like your sister Jill."

"Oh, no!" said Molly. "Your hair is so pretty
the way it is! It looks like a . . . like a coppery-gold
waterfall, if there could be such a thing." Molly
turned to a page in the scrapbook that had family
pictures. She pointed to a photograph of Emily.
"Look how shiny your hair looks in this photograph
of you at—where is this? Windsor Castle, where the
princesses live? What are you and this tall man doing
with the shovels?"

Emily didn't answer right away. As she looked
at the photograph, her heart hurt a little bit with
homesickness again. When she did answer, she made
her voice sound steady, but her explanation came
out in short sentences. "That's my grandfather and
me," she said. "And that's not Windsor Castle. That's
my grandparents' house. Grandy and I are planting

a tree. We planted one every year on my birthday. Grandy loves trees and gardens."

"That's your grandparents' *house?*" asked Molly. She whistled. "It's huge. Do they live there all alone?"

"No," said Emily. "When the war began, Grandy invited a boys' school evacuated from London to use their house. The boys and their teachers live there with Grandmum and Grandy."

"That's nice of your grandparents," said Molly.

"Grandy says we must all do all we can to help England win the war," Emily said. "He was in the Royal Navy during the last war, and he gave me his dog tags when I left to come here. Look."

Emily slipped her hand under the pillow on her bed and pulled out the red and green dog tags strung on a silk ribbon. She put them into Molly's hand.

British dog tags

"My dad has dog tags, too, with his name and identification stuff on them," said Molly. "He's a doctor in the Army."

"My dad's a doctor, too!" said Emily, happy to have found something else in common with Molly besides puns and princesses. It encouraged her to say something that was important to her and to trust that Molly would understand. "Grandy said that he was giving me his dog tags because they'd remind me to be brave and to help England," Emily said carefully. "I hate to be a disappointment to him. But I don't see how I can be brave and help England way over here in America."

"Well," said Molly comfortingly, "I think you're brave *because* you're here, so far from home." She looked at the dog tags thoughtfully. Then she said, "I tell you what. Wear the dog tags around your neck. That way they'll remind you to be on the lookout all the time for ways to be brave and to help England." Molly rose to her knees and slipped the looped ribbon over Emily's head so that the dog tags hung like a necklace. "And I'll be on the lookout for you, too."

Emily liked the way the dog tags felt. They were a gentle weight on her chest. "Thank you, Molly," she said.

"Thank *you* for the math help," said Molly. As she climbed into bed, she said, "You know, Emily, I think it is going to be absolutely great having you here."

Emily smiled. This time it was as clear as the

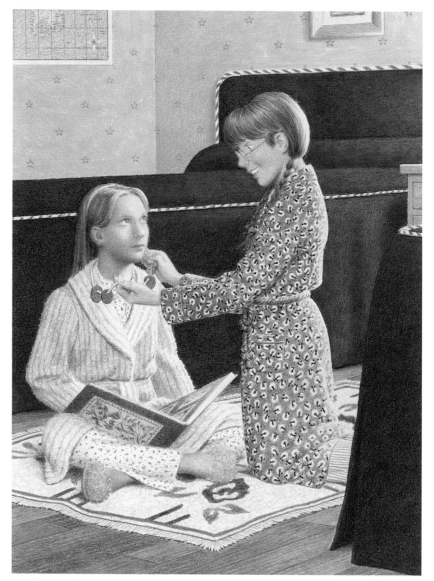

"Wear the dog tags around your neck," said Molly. "That way they'll remind you to be on the lookout for ways to be brave and to help England."

bright starry sky outside the window that her just-beginning friend Molly meant what she said. *Absolutely.*

467 Oak Street
Jefferson, Illinois, U.S.A.
Thurs., 30 March, 1944

Dear Mum and Dad,

How are you? I am very well, thank you. Molly and I are beginning to be friends. She likes puns, too, Dad!

Tell Grandy that Molly is going to help me find a way to be brave and help England all the way over here in America.

Isn't that sporting of her?

Love and many, many kisses,
Cheerio!
Emily

CHAPTER TWO

HOT CROSS BUNS

 Emily knew the truth about herself. She was *not* brave. She only pretended to be brave and even that was hard for her to do. She had been sure that nothing could be harder than acting brave when waving good-bye to Mum and Dad in London, not knowing when she'd see them again, and watching out the train window as they shrank smaller and smaller until they disappeared. Nothing could be harder than acting brave while she was on the huge, gray ship from England as it slunk sneakily across the endless, cold ocean, in constant danger of being sunk by German torpedoes. Nothing could be harder than acting brave when she stumbled exhausted off

the bus in Jefferson, expecting to be scooped up into the familiar arms of Aunt Primrose—only to be met by Mrs. McIntire, who, though very nice, was a complete stranger. Emily had thought nothing could be harder than acting brave when Mrs. McIntire took her home to a house confusingly full of noise and children where everything was new and different to her.

But she had been wrong. Hardest by far had been acting brave last Monday—the first day she went to school with Molly. Emily hated being the center of attention. So she'd gone stiff with shy self-consciousness when the children crowded around her. She'd kept her answers to their questions clipped and short. Even so, the children repeated what she said, imitating her accent so that she'd feared that they were making fun of her. She hadn't really known how to answer their questions anyway. How could she possibly describe to Molly and her friends, who were so safe and carefree and comfortable, how terrible it was to sleep underground in a tube station, or to see a house bombed, or a bus explode, or to be always cold? If she told the truth, she'd sound like a

complaining crybaby. Grandy had said that she must always remember that she was British, and that the British never complain. They "grin and bear it."

But sometimes grinning and bearing it felt as dishonest as pretending to be brave. Take this morning, for example. Emily skipped downstairs to breakfast happy because of her talk with Molly the night before, happy because it was end-of-the-school-week Friday, and happy because she was wearing a pretty spring frock and cardigan that Aunt Primrose had had delivered for her. But when she sat at the table, her happiness collapsed.

"Oatmeal?" Ricky groaned, expressing every-one's dismay. "We've had that sticky old stuff every day this week. Do we have to have it again?"

"Yes," said Mrs. Gilford firmly. "We want our guest, Emily, to have what she likes, and oatmeal's the breakfast she's used to at home in England. Isn't that right, Emily?"

Emily was torn. Mrs. Gilford was partly right; because eggs, buttered toast, jam, and bacon were in short supply, Emily had had oatmeal for breakfast every morning since rationing had begun, four years ago. But Mrs. Gilford was also wrong. Emily had never particularly liked oatmeal to begin with, and now she was heartily sick of it. But Emily knew that it would be rude to say so. Mum's note told her to be good, tidy, obedient, and honest while in America, but most of all to be polite and grateful. And so Emily said, "Yes, quite, thank you, Mrs. Gilford," and ate her oatmeal.

She could feel Jill, Ricky, and Molly looking at her unhappily. Emily didn't blame them, and she was very sorry to do anything that might jeopardize her just-beginning friendship with Molly. She wanted to hug Brad when he manfully ate a big spoonful of oatmeal and said stoutly, "Well, *I* like it."

"Well, *I* don't," said Ricky flatly.

Mrs. Gilford glared, but Ricky was undaunted. Emily was always a little shocked at how outspoken American children were, and the rather cheeky way they blurted out what they were thinking. She watched, fascinated, as Ricky poured so much milk on his oatmeal that it was twice her daily milk ration in England. Then he nonchalantly helped himself to a banana, sliced that onto his oatmeal, and proceeded to eat the bowlful of what now looked like a banana float. Bananas were an exotic fruit to Emily. They had not been available in England for so many years that once, when a girl had one, she brought it to school so that all the children could see it and smell it.

"Would you like more oatmeal, Emily?" Mrs. Gilford asked.

Emily summoned her grit. "Thank you, no, Mrs. Gilford," she said politely. "I had better not. In England, there are big posters everywhere that say, 'Don't take more than you can eat.'"

"Very wise," said Mrs. Gilford with approval.

"It wouldn't work with me," said Ricky breezily. "In my case, I always want to *eat* more than I'm allowed to *take!*"

Everyone laughed at Ricky's wisecrack, even Mrs. Gilford.

★

On the playground after lunch that day, Emily and Molly were playing hopscotch with Molly's two friends, Linda and Susan.

"Emily," Susan sighed, "I love your new dress! Cherries and cherry blossoms! Twirl so we can see!"

Emily turned timidly in a small circle and Susan *oohed* and *ahhed* ecstatically. Emily was embarrassed by the attention, but she was a little pleased, too. Clothing was rationed in England, and it had been a long time since she had had a dress that was brand-new. She was shyly proud to have her dress admired.

Even level-headed Linda was approving. "I like that cardigan," she said to Emily. "It looks good unbuttoned. You know, when you first got here, you wore your sweater buttoned up to your chin. You looked cold all the time. You *acted* sort of cold, too, and standoffish."

"Not standoffish, just standbackish!" softhearted Susan said quickly. "And anyway, we were glad you weren't a show-off."

"I guess it took a little time for us to get used to you and how you're English," said Molly. "And it took time for you to get used to us and how we're American, right?"

"Quite right," said Emily.

"Quite right!" echoed Molly, Linda, and Susan, cheerfully.

Emily felt cheerful, too, and as warmed by the girls' sunny friendliness as she was by the bright spring sunshine. She now knew that the girls weren't making fun of the way she spoke. They were just being playful when they repeated what she said. Also, Emily was an observant girl. She had noticed that Molly was thoroughly good-natured, that Susan was never unkind, and that although blunt Linda didn't soften the truth, she never poked fun at anyone but herself.

The bell rang. As the girls went inside to their classroom, Emily wondered. *Was* she getting used to Americans? She was still taken aback by how large, loud, rowdy, and rambunctious the children were. Her school in England had girls only, so she was especially unaccustomed to boys' boisterousness. Just now, the boys were tossing a wadded-up ball of paper from desk to desk, even though the teacher, Miss Campbell, had clapped her hands for order.

"Boys and girls, I am waiting," said Miss Campbell.

Emily sat up straight and silent. She wanted Miss Campbell to like her as much as she wanted Molly and Molly's friends to like her. Emily was rewarded with a smile from Miss Campbell and, much to her surprise, a wink. In Emily's experience, teachers in England never winked at students!

"I see that we have one good citizen in our classroom this afternoon," said Miss Campbell. "Emily is ready."

When, eventually, all the children were quiet, Miss Campbell began the lesson. She asked, "Who can tell me some of the ways that children on the home front support our soldiers fighting in the war?" Almost every hand in the room shot up. Miss Campbell called on Alison Hargate.

"We collect scrap metal and paper and rubber," said Alison, "so that they can be used to make weapons and things the soldiers need."

"We buy war stamps," added Howie Munson, "and take plane-identification classes so that we can tell if planes are ours or an enemy's."

"We help the Red Cross pack boxes of books and warm blankets to send to the soldiers," said Molly.

"We're careful not to waste food or clothes or electricity," said Linda.

"Or hot water," Woody Halsey called out. "That's why I never take a bath anymore!"

"Ewww!" everyone howled delightedly.

Woody's joke was met with such uproarious laughter that Howie Munson jumped up from his seat and pretended to scrub Woody with imaginary soap. Woody pretended to shampoo his hair, which made the class laugh even louder.

"Please be seated, Howie," said Miss Campbell. "You, too, Woody. Class, settle down, please."

When order was restored, Miss Campbell said, "When we support our soldiers in all the ways that you mentioned, we are being *patriotic*." Miss Campbell wrote "patriotic" on the blackboard. "Who can tell me some things that make us feel patriotic?"

"The flag," said Molly enthusiastically. Everyone nodded.

"President Roosevelt on the radio," said Grace Littlefield, "and pictures of Mrs. Roosevelt in the newspaper, visiting wounded soldiers."

"Newsreels of battleships and tanks," said a boy named Josh.

"Excellent answers," said Miss Campbell. "You have your thinking caps on this afternoon, I can see." Then she asked, "How about you, Emily? Can you tell us something that makes people in both England *and* America feel patriotic?"

Everyone turned to look at Emily. She was so eager to answer well that her heart thumped like a drum. Suddenly, Emily brightened. "Music," she said. "Marching bands and military music always make people feel patriotic."

Emily was pleased when everyone murmured in agreement with her answer.

Miss Campbell beamed. "Splendid!" she said. "Just the answer I was looking for. Music makes us feel patriotic when we hear it, or sing it, or play it on an instrument. And that is why—" Miss Campbell paused and looked at the children with sparkling eyes before she went on, "our PTA here at Willow Street School has decided that every member of our class is going to be given a musical instrument on loan. It's called a *Flutophone* and it's like a clarinet. You'll eventually learn how to play patriotic songs on it!"

"Hurray!" cheered the class. Emily, feeling loose and daring, cheered, too. She was just as excited as everyone else, though she did not go as far as Howie

Flutophone Munson and Woody Halsey, who stood up and pretended that their hands were clarinets,

25

wiggling their fingers wildly as they played pretend keys and made tootling sounds.

"Look at us!" said Howie. "We're going to be great at the Flutophones!"

Miss Campbell laughed tolerantly. "We'll just see how well you do with the real thing!" she said, starting to hand out the Flutophones.

By the end of the afternoon, Emily noticed that Miss Campbell was not laughing anymore. Her hair, which was usually smooth and tidy, had frizzed to frazzled wisps around her face, and her face looked frazzled, too. Miss Campbell had told the children not to play their Flutophones until she had finished handing them all out and had demonstrated how to play them correctly. But the Flutophones were so wonderfully sleek and new that no one could resist just one little toot, and so the classroom was filled with a cacophony of blasts, honks, squeaks, and the occasional ear-splitting screech. Many of the children seemed to be under the impression that the harder they blew, the better. Their screeches, which were especially ear-splitting, were accompanied by a chorus of children yelling at them to cut it out. Miss Campbell finally had to flick the lights for order, since no one could hear her over the ruckus.

Over and over again, Miss Campbell showed the children where to place their fingers on the Flutophone in order to play "Hot Cross Buns."

Emily was glad "Hot Cross Buns" was their first song, because she knew the tune already. She watched and listened diligently as Miss Campbell patiently showed the children how to follow the

hot cross buns

notes printed on their sheet music. Emily couldn't hear her own playing very well, but it seemed to her that hardly anyone was hitting the right note at the right time.

"Well," said Miss Campbell when the children lined up to go home, "I think we can all agree that it's going to take a lot of practice."

"You can say that again!" said Linda.

"I'm going to give you practice cards as you leave," said Miss Campbell. "I want you to write down how much time you practice your Flutophone every day, so that you can keep track of it. Ask a grownup

27

to sign your cards. In a week or two, I'll check your cards to see how much you have practiced. Remember, practice makes perfect!"

Emily folded her sheet music and neatly tucked her practice cards inside it. Then she and Molly, Linda, and Susan practically flew out the door of the school. They could not *wait* to get to Molly's house to play their Flutophones. The girls rushed into the kitchen all abuzz with excited self-importance.

"Look!" said Molly. All four girls held up their Flutophones to show Mrs. Gilford.

"What're those?" asked Mrs. Gilford.

"Flutophones!" said Molly.

Mrs. Gilford said, "Just what we need," which Emily recognized as an example of an American saying the exact opposite of what she meant.

"Listen!" said Molly. The girls began to play, more or less together.

But they had played only three notes before Mrs. Gilford held up her hand to stop them. "What are you doing?" she asked.

"Why, playing 'Hot Cross Buns,' of course," said Molly.

Mrs. Gilford raised her eyebrows, looking

unconvinced. "Take an apple for a snack, each of you," she said. "Then take your phono-fluto-foona-floats to the garage. Play them out there, not in here. Off you go, lickety-split."

The four girls took their apples and climbed up the stairs to the little room over the McIntires' garage. Their enthusiasm was only the tiniest bit cooled by Mrs. Gilford's chilly reaction to their playing.

"I know what," said Molly. "This time, let's take turns."

"Yes," said Linda. "Maybe it'll sound better."

"You go first, Emily, because you are the guest," Susan said graciously.

"Oh, dear me, no!" said Emily, pink cheeked. She didn't want the girls to hear how poorly she played. They'd think she was pitiful! "I can't play at all well yet."

"Are you kidding?" Linda asked. "We *all* stink."

"Don't worry, Emily," said Molly more kindly. "We're all just beginners."

Emily did not want to let Molly down. So she took a deep breath and very slowly, she played her Flutophone, singing the song in her head:

Hot cross buns,
Hot cross buns,
One a penny,
Two a penny,
Hot cross buns.

When she finished, Molly, Linda, and Susan stared at her in such shocked silence that Emily trembled. Then, suddenly, the three girls surprised Emily by bursting into applause.

"Gosh," gushed Susan. "That was great, Emily."

"Yes!" agreed Linda. "Can you read music? Because I could actually tell that you were playing 'Hot Cross Buns.'"

Molly smiled at Emily as if she was proud of her. "Music!" she said. "Here's *another* thing you're good at, Emily, just like you're good at math."

"And at being neat and tidy and proper and ladylike," Susan listed.

Emily smiled, but uncertainly. The girls' praise made her feel a little nervous. She really wasn't musical at all. All she knew about reading music came from singing hymns in church, where she'd

The three girls surprised Emily by bursting into applause.

learned that if the notes went up on the lines of the staff, that meant her voice should go up, too. The fact that she could play "Hot Cross Buns" was just a Flutophone fluke. She tried to tell the girls. "Well, thank you," she began, "but I'm really—"

"You're really *good!*" Molly interrupted, waving away Emily's protests.

"You won't say so because you're just being a 'not-a-show-off' again, as usual," added Susan.

"You're a million trillion times better than we are," Linda exaggerated. "If you don't believe it, just listen to me."

Linda began to play, so Emily didn't have a chance to insist that the girls were wrong, that, as Molly would say, she *absolutely* was *not* good at music. But the secret truth was that in her heart of hearts, Emily did not want to disillusion the girls. It felt so wonderful to bask in their warm admiration! It made Emily feel like a full-fledged friend for the first time.

And after all, Emily said to herself, *if I let them think I'm good at music, I'm only exaggerating a little, like Americans do. What harm can there be in that?*

467 Oak Street
    Jefferson, Illinois, U.S.A.
      Friday, 31 March, 1944

Dear Mum and Dad,

    How are you? I am fine. Guess what? Today all the children in our class were given flutophones. Here is a pun for you, Dad: I hope you like my notes. ♩♪♪ As my friend Molly would say, Get it?

           Love, Emily

P.S. Please tell Grandy that I won't forget. Molly and I will try to find a way for me to be brave and help England.

CHAPTER THREE

PRACTICE MAKES PERFECT

 Emily had taken her grandfather's words very much to heart. Every night, ever since she had arrived in America, Emily had slipped Grandy's dog tags under her pillow before she went to sleep and hoped that the next day she would find a way to be brave and help England. She was glad to wear Grandy's dog tags all day as a reminder to be "on the lookout," as Molly had said. But it was hard to find a way to help England, because she was so swept up in her American life. There was school, homework, helping Molly with multiplication, house chores, and working in the Victory garden. And now that it seemed as though Molly, Linda, and Susan wanted

her to be their friend, Emily would have even less time, because she wanted to spend as much time as possible with them.

The four girls got together every day over the weekend to practice their Flutophones. They were enthusiastic on Friday afternoon and practiced for forty-five minutes. They were conscientious on Saturday and practiced for half an hour. They were frankly a little bored by Sunday and eked out only fifteen minutes of practice before they went outside to jump rope.

"Don't you hope Miss Campbell teaches us a new song to play today?" Molly asked Emily as they went to breakfast Monday morning.

Actually, Emily dreaded the thought of a new song because it would reveal that she'd fudged her playing and that it was just pure luck that she was able to play "Hot Cross Buns" on the Flutophone. But she didn't want Molly to know that. So she joked in her quiet way. "Do you mean to say that you're fed up with 'Hot Cross Buns'?" she asked. "You're not hoping that Mrs. Gilford serves some for breakfast?"

"That's right!" chortled Molly. "I'm almost *glad* it'll be oatmeal!"

After breakfast, which was indeed grin-and-bear-it oatmeal again, the girls presented their practice cards to Mrs. Gilford. "I'll take your word for it that you practiced as much as you've written here," said Mrs. Gilford, who had held firm about no Flutophone playing in the house. "I'm happy to say I didn't hear you floo-tootling one toot." She signed, the girls thanked her, and then they skipped off to school, Flutophones in hand.

The first thing Miss Campbell said was, "Boys and girls! I am going to ask you to put your Flutophones in your desks and leave them there. I don't want to see anyone fiddling with a Flutophone until it is time for our lesson after lunch."

The children obeyed, and Miss Campbell started the lesson.

"In science we learned about how animals disguise themselves so that they can hide from their predators," said Miss Campbell. "Who can tell me how that idea is put to use by our troops?"

"It's camouflage," Molly piped up. "Soldiers wear green uniforms and put leaves on their helmets so that they'll blend in with the trees."

"Ships and tanks are camouflaged,

too," added Howie, "to hide them from the enemy."
He turned to Emily and asked, "Was your ship from
England camouflaged?"

Emily nodded. She shivered, too, remembering
how frightened she had been on the dark, gloomy
ship with its slippery decks and sinister guns.
Grandy, who had been in the Royal Navy, wouldn't
think that she had been brave for England when
she was on the ship! "The ship was gray," she said
in a small voice, "so it wouldn't stand out and be
noticeable on the ocean."

"Thank you, Emily," said Miss Campbell.
"Speaking of noticing, I am disappointed to notice
that you're having trouble leaving your Flutophone
alone, Woody. Evidently I'll have to take care of it
for you until it's time for our lesson. Please bring
it to me now."

Emily was relieved that the class's attention had
shifted away from her to Woody as he went up to
Miss Campbell's desk, shamefaced, and handed over
his Flutophone. "Now, let's get back to work," said
Miss Campbell briskly.

When it was time for their Flutophone lesson,
Emily saw Molly, Linda, and Susan put their heads

together and whisper. Then Linda and Susan glanced at Emily, struggling to hide their smiles, and Molly raised her hand.

"Miss Campbell," said Molly, "Emily can play 'Hot Cross Buns' really well. You should hear her."

Emily shrank in her seat as every face in the room turned to look at her. Molly nodded and said encouragingly, "Show everybody, Emily."

Oh, dear me, no! thought Emily.

But Miss Campbell said, "Please stand and play for us, Emily." And Emily had to do as she was told. She stood on wobbly legs and began to blow, singing "Hot Cross Buns" in her head as before. Her playing was as wobbly as her legs, but somehow she managed to hit the right notes. When she finished, Emily felt weak and out of breath, as if she'd run a long race.

Everyone clapped, Molly beamed, and Miss Campbell said, "Splendid!"

Emily didn't feel splendid. Now the whole class, and Miss Campbell, too, thought she was good at music. The little misunderstanding was multiplying out of control! What would everyone think of her when they found out that she was a fake? And they were sure to find out soon, because Miss Campbell began to teach a new song, called "America the Beautiful," which Emily had never heard before. Fortunately for Emily, everyone played the new song so terribly that her wrong notes were lost in the confusion.

"Practice," Miss Campbell reminded the children sternly when they lined up to go home. "Remember—"

The whole class said aloud with her, "Practice makes perfect."

But Emily couldn't practice after school with Molly, Linda, and Susan because they had tap-dancing lessons at Miss LaVonda's.

"Come with us, Emily," Molly urged. She and Linda and Susan demonstrated a few tap-dancing steps on the sidewalk outside school. "Tap dancing is fun. You'll like it."

"We're going to have lessons every day after school this week," Susan added, bouncing on her toes with excitement, "because we're going to put on a show at a War Bond rally really soon! If you come to lessons, I bet Miss LaVonda will let you dance in the show, too. Come on."

Emily shuddered. Even though she wanted to be with her new friends, the thought of tap dancing and, worse, performing in front of strangers, made her blood run cold with horror. Nothing could induce her to grin and bear *that*. "No, thank you," she said, politely but definitely. "I shan't."

"Okay," said Molly. "See you later at home." She and Linda and Susan waved their Flutophones and said, "Bye!"

"Good-bye!" Emily answered. She scurried off in a homeward direction, grateful that she'd have a chance to practice her Flutophone all by herself for a while. She desperately wanted to see if she could figure out the tune of "America the Beautiful" so that she wouldn't sound terrible in front of Molly.

As soon as Emily changed out of her school clothes, she went to the room above the garage to practice. Brad, bringing graham crackers for a snack, joined her to keep her company. Somehow, Emily didn't mind sounding terrible in front of him. Brad thought everything she did was just right. He sat on the floor eating his graham crackers and listened intently as she huffed and puffed and struggled through the tune.

After a while, sweaty and discouraged, Emily stopped for a graham cracker break. She asked Brad, "How long do you think I've been practicing?"

"A hundred minutes?" suggested Brad, who couldn't tell time.

Emily was far too kind to hurt Brad's feelings, so she didn't contradict him although she knew perfectly well that she had been practicing closer to twenty minutes than a hundred, even if it *felt* like a hundred *hours*. She stood up and brushed cracker crumbs off her shirt. "Let's go look at the clock in the kitchen," she said.

"Okay," said Brad agreeably.

The kitchen clock confirmed that in fact Emily had been practicing for a scant fifteen minutes. Emily's face fell. "That's not very long," she said. She wrote the number 15 on her practice card, thinking how skimpy it looked.

"Don't worry, Emily," said Brad. "You can practice more when Molly comes home. Want to go help Mrs. Gilford in the garden?"

"Jolly good!" said Emily. She left her Flutophone and practice card on the kitchen table and followed Brad outside. It was such a beautiful spring day! No one, Emily thought, could blame her for not going back inside the dank garage, even though a teeny tiny voice nagged at her, saying that she should practice more to plump up that fifteen minutes.

"Would you like to help me plant this lettuce?" Mrs. Gilford asked when Emily and Brad appeared to help her.

"Yes, indeed," said Emily as she knelt in the dirt.

"Me, too," said Brad.

Emily and Brad both liked helping Mrs. Gilford in the Victory garden. Brad liked it because he was very fond of worms, sticks, puddles, and any excuse to get dirty. Emily liked it because it reminded her of working with Mum in their little garden in London and with Grandy in his much bigger garden at his house outside of London. Mrs. Gilford's gardening outfit was even the same as Grandy's. They both wore stiff straw hats, thick gardening gloves, and knee-high black rubber boots. Emily also liked the smell of the cool earth and the feeling of the sturdy little seedlings in her hands. She enjoyed the sense that there was a lot going on in a garden, lots of things *beginning,* although you couldn't see all of them because they were quietly going about

their growing underground.

"You eat lettuce in England, don't you?" Mrs. Gilford asked Emily.

"Oh yes, in tea sandwiches, on special occasions," said Emily. "We put it on thin bread, with mayonnaise." She corrected herself. "That is, we *used* to. The only bread we have now is National Loaf. It tastes dreadful, and it's hard to slice thin. And mayonnaise is made from eggs, and eggs are hard to come by now, because of the war."

"You can have my eggs, Emily," said Brad, "and send them to England."

"Thank you, Brad," said Emily seriously. "It's kind of you to offer. But I'm afraid the eggs might get broken on the way. So I think you had better eat them here, or they'll be wasted."

Emily smiled at Brad, wishing that she *could* send eggs home, or even ask the Red Cross to send turnips, as Molly had joked. Sending food would be a way to help England. But Emily knew that even if it were possible, Brad's eggs and Molly's turnips would have to be magically multiplied to make a difference.

Mrs. Gilford stood up. "That's enough for today," she said. "Time to get ready for dinner. Brad, wash off at the garden hose before you go inside. You've got to leave some of the dirt in the garden, else nothing will grow!"

★

Emily had just finished setting the table for dinner when Molly came dancing home from her lesson. "Emily," she asked, "have you practiced your Flutophone yet?"

"A bit," said Emily.

"Oh, good!" said Molly. "Because Linda and

Susan and I practiced at Miss LaVonda's. I hope you don't mind."

"Not at all," said Emily honestly. She was secretly relieved.

She was even more relieved when Molly went on to say, "I think we'll practice our Flutophones at Miss LaVonda's every day this week. It gives us something to do while we wait for our part in the rehearsal. Is that okay with you?"

"Yes, indeed," said Emily.

Molly grinned. "We're not anywhere near as good as you are, anyway," she said. "We'd just hold you back."

Emily knew that this was the moment to tell Molly the truth. She plucked up her courage and plunged. "Molly," she began, "I—"

But Molly interrupted her. "It was so wonderful the way you played 'Hot Cross Buns' in front of everybody at school today, Emily," Molly said. "I just wanted to shout out and brag to the whole world, 'That's Emily! She's my friend and boy, am I glad she is! Isn't she *great?*'"

Emily smiled weakly.

"Look!" said Molly. "I even wrote your parents

a letter about it."

Emily felt cold all over as she read Molly's letter to Mum and Dad. The misunderstanding was multiplying faster than the nine times tables! There was no question about it. She could not possibly tell Molly the truth *now*.

Monday, April 3, 1944

Dear Dr. and Mrs. Bennett,
    Hi! I am Emily's American friend, Molly. Everyone here thinks that Emily is a very nice girl. She was shy at first. She was very, very quiet. But then we got flutophones, and now Emily is the star ⭐ ⭐ ⭐ of our class! I am so proud that she is my friend!

    Love,
    Molly McIntire
P.S. Emily is good at multiplication, too! She taught me that 5, 6, 7, 8 is a way to remember $56 = 7 \times 8$. Isn't that great?

CHAPTER FOUR

$45 \times 10 = 450$

"Whenever you multiply a number by ten, just put a zero on the end of it," Emily explained to Molly as the two girls were walking along the sunny sidewalk to school on Friday morning. "Two times ten is 2-0, or 20. Five times ten is 5-0, or fifty. And it even works with double-digit numbers, Molly. Fifty-six times ten is 5-6-0, or 560."

Molly slapped her forehead with her hand. "That's so easy!" she said.

"Quite," said Emily. "Now the rule for eleven only works with single digits. When you multiply a number by eleven, the answer is that number twice. Five times eleven is 5-5, or 55—"

"Eight times eleven is 8-8, or 88," Molly cut in. "That's really easy, too!"

"Yup!" said Emily. She thought she sounded very American; after all, she had been in America for nearly two weeks!

"Emily," Molly said with a happy skip, "you are the best person I have ever known at math. You make multiplying easy."

Emily beamed and skipped quite happily, too. If only she could find a way to multiply the minutes she spent practicing her Flutophone, she thought, she'd be *absolutely* happy.

Emily was a conscientious girl. Every day after school that week, she had doggedly hooted and tootled on her Flutophone for as long as she could stand it. But unfortunately, she could never stand it longer than fifteen minutes. Miss Campbell said that practice made perfect, but it didn't seem to make *anything* in Emily's case. She never seemed to get any better. Her only consolation was that it didn't seem to matter too much. At school, with everyone honking away together, it seemed to Emily that it was impossible to tell who was playing well and who wasn't.

So Emily was very surprised that afternoon when, during their Flutophone lesson, Miss Campbell stopped everyone and said, "I think someone is out of tune with the rest of the class."

"It's Emily-from-England," said Woody. "I'm next to her, so I can tell."

Emily couldn't breathe, she was so embarrassed.

Then Howie made it worse by teasing Emily in front of everyone. "Hey, Miss Pied Piper," he said. "I thought you were good at flutophoning."

"She is!" said Molly hotly. "You be quiet, Howie. You, too, Woody."

"Just ignore those silly old boys, Emily," Susan murmured.

"Yes," said Linda. "They hardly know which end of their Flutophones to blow into."

Howie, who was always game for a laugh, turned his Flutophone upside down and blew into the wrong end.

Everyone giggled.

Miss Campbell crossed her arms. "Excuse me, boys and girls," she said sharply. "I don't remember giving permission to talk. Talking will not make our music sound better. Let's take it from the top again.

All together, now. Everyone, *begin*."

But Emily was too mortified to play. For the rest of the lesson, she just held her Flutophone to her lips, puffed out her cheeks, moved her fingers over the keys, and pretended. She went limp with relief when Miss Campbell finally dismissed the class.

"I want all of you to promise me that you'll practice twice as long as usual over this weekend," Miss Campbell said as the children lined up to file out the door. "I want 'America the Beautiful' to *be* beautiful by Monday."

"Yes, Miss Campbell," Emily said along with all the other children.

She really meant it, too. Emily was determined to practice more, even if it meant that she had to face the music and reveal how badly she played to Molly, Linda, and Susan when they practiced together over the weekend.

But as it turned out, Molly, Linda, and Susan had tap-dancing rehearsal all day Saturday. And on Sunday, Mrs. McIntire and Emily went to the hospital to visit Aunt Primrose. So somehow or other, the four girls did not practice together over the weekend. Emily practiced alone as usual, with only

Brad to hear how badly she played. And on Monday, Tuesday, and Wednesday, she practiced alone after school. Every morning, when Emily looked at her practice card before she took it to Mrs. Gilford to sign, she was sorry but not surprised to see that despite her good intentions, the amount of time she'd practiced her Flutophone was fifteen skinny minutes.

Thursday was a rainy day, so after lunch the class had indoor recess in the gymnasium. Molly, Linda, and Susan demonstrated for Emily the tap dance they were rehearsing at Miss LaVonda's. They hummed the music and tapped and twirled, and spun and whirled along with their humming.

When they finished their dance, Emily clapped hard.

"It's even better when we have our tap shoes on," said Susan breathlessly, "and when we have our cymbals and triangle and tambourine to play."

"I think your dance is very good, very good indeed," Emily said.

"I think it's very short, very *short* indeed," said Linda crankily. "If the audience blinks, they'll miss it altogether."

"Well, look on the bright side," said Susan. "Since our part of the show is so short, we've had lots and lots of time to practice our Flutophones during rehearsals."

"Lots and lots of time?" Emily asked.

"Yup," said Molly. "And it's a good thing we've had Miss LaVonda's assistant sign our practice cards for us. Miss Campbell told me that she's going to check our cards today to see how much we've practiced."

Emily tried to sound calm. "How much have you three been practicing?" she asked the girls.

"Oh, *hours* every day," said Linda.

"Hours?" asked Emily in a quavery voice.

Molly, Linda, and Susan all nodded. "Sure," they said breezily. Then they went back to tap dancing, their feet making a nice satisfactory pounding sound on the wooden gymnasium floor.

Emily's heart was pounding, too. *Oh dear, oh dear!* she thought. *They have practiced for hours. I am sure that everyone else in the class has, too—everyone except me! When Molly finds out that I've only practiced fifteen minutes a day, she'll realize that Woody was right;*

I'm terrible at the Flutophone. I've been tricking her. She certainly won't want to brag that I am her friend then. Oh, what shall I do?

When the dancers' backs were turned, Emily slipped out of the gymnasium. She slithered like a snake through the winding hallways and into Miss Campbell's classroom. It was shadowy inside the classroom, which was so eerily empty and quiet that it felt spooky. With shaky hands, Emily took her practice card out of her desk. Quickly, she changed all the 1s to 4s, so that it looked like she'd practiced not 15, but 45 minutes a day for the last ten days. Just as the rest of the class came in, Emily slid her card into her desk.

"Hey, Emily, you disappeared from the gymnasium," said Molly. "How come?"

"I came back early," said Emily unsteadily, "to, uh, to do some math."

"Yikes, when you didn't *have* to?" Molly said with a grin. "You *do* like numbers, don't you?"

Emily grinned back a watery grin. She seemed to hear her own voice telling Molly days ago that she liked numbers because they never lied. And now she had made the numbers on her practice card do just that.

"Pass your practice cards forward, please, boys and girls," Miss Campbell was saying. "I will look at them while you do pages 89 and 90 in your math workbooks. Quietly, please!"

Emily's heart was thudding so loudly that she thought that Miss Campbell must have been speaking to her specifically when she asked for quiet. The workbook pages were a blur and Emily, who usually breezed through math problems, was so distracted by worry that she was only halfway done when Miss Campbell said, "Close your workbooks, boys and girls. Any problems you haven't finished must be done for homework."

The students put their workbooks away and Miss Campbell wrote on the blackboard:

"Who can do this multiplication for me?" Miss Campbell asked.

"Four hundred fifty!" Molly hollered out before anyone else even raised his hand.

"My goodness, Molly!" said Miss Campbell, pleased. "It's clear to see that you have been studying your multiplication tables."

"Emily's been helping me," said Molly, beaming with pride for herself and for Emily.

"Has she?" said Miss Campbell. "We are lucky to have Emily in our class." Miss Campbell gave Emily one of her friendly winks. Then she said, "Boys and girls, I am proud to announce that one student in our class practiced the Flutophone more than anyone else. This student practiced forty-five minutes a day for the last ten days, or—"

"Four hundred fifty minutes!" everyone shouted

out at the same time.

"Correct," said Miss Campbell.

"Who did it?" asked Linda.

Miss Campbell smiled a special smile. "Emily," she said simply.

"Hurray!" cheered all the students. "Yay, Emily!"

"And Emily was good to begin with!" Molly boasted.

Emily went rigid. *How on earth did this happen?* she wondered. Then, in a sickening flash, she understood. Linda had only been kidding when she'd said that she and Molly and Susan had practiced for hours. Once again, Emily had misunderstood an American exaggeration.

Just when Emily thought that things could not get worse, Miss Campbell went on. "I have a wonderful surprise," Miss Campbell said. "On Saturday evening, our class is going to present a program for the rest of the school and the PTA. You will play 'America the Beautiful' on your Flutophones. And, because she practiced the most, who do you think will play a solo?"

"EMILY!" everyone exclaimed.

"Yes," said Miss Campbell. She started to clap

for Emily, and all the students joined in, clapping and cheering and stamping their feet.

This was the worst moment of Emily's life so far. "Oh no! Please!" she gasped, hot and pink in the face. "I can't do it. Truly, I can't."

But everyone was clapping so hard, nobody heard Emily but Susan. "Good old Emily!" Susan said to her fondly. "Trying to be a 'not-a-show-off' again, as usual!"

With all her heart, Emily wished that she were back on the ship in the middle of the Atlantic Ocean! German torpedoes were nowhere near as terrible as the trap she'd gotten herself into. She would humiliate herself by playing badly, and then *everyone*—the whole school and the PTA—would know that she was a fake and a fraud and . . . Emily swallowed hard . . . a liar. Now *no* one would ever want to be her friend.

Oh, thought Emily hopelessly, *what, oh what, can I do?*

★

Emily was far too unhappy to sleep that night. She didn't want Molly to hear her crying, so she slid her hand under her pillow, gathered Grandy's dog tags in her hand, and tiptoed down the stairs and outside. Emily flew across the driveway to the garage and ran up the stairs to the little room above. She sat on the floor and wept.

"Hey," someone whispered.

Emily turned. It was Molly. Emily swiped her cheeks with her hands, but Molly had already seen her tears.

"I thought you might be cold and need this," Molly said. She sat down, draped Emily's bathrobe over Emily's shoulders, and then left her arm around Emily. "What's the matter?" Molly asked. "Are you homesick?"

Emily shook her head. "It's worse than that," she said.

"What?" asked Molly.

"I lied," said Emily.

"Oh," said Molly softly.

Miserably, Emily poured out her whole story. "I can't play the Flutophone," she said. "I never could. I hated practicing so much that I only practiced fifteen minutes a day. Then today, you and Linda and Susan told me that you had been practicing for hours every day—"

"We were kidding!" said Molly. "That was just an exaggeration."

"But I believed you," said Emily. "I guess I'm still not used to the way Americans joke and exaggerate. Anyway, I was so ashamed  that I changed all the 1s on my practice card to 4s so that it would look as if I'd practiced 45 minutes every day, instead of 15. I didn't know that would also make it look as if I'd practiced more than anyone else in the class."

"Whoosh," exhaled Molly. "You changed the 1s to 4s? That was a pretty daring thing to do."

"Daring?" repeated Emily. "No, not daring. It was just desperate—and stupid. I was so afraid that if you found out that I wasn't good at the Flutophone, you'd be disappointed in me, just like Grandy's disappointed that I'm not brave and I'm not helping England. I pretended to be good at the Flutophone just like I pretended to be brave. I've been a fake about everything. I even pretended to like oatmeal! And now I'm a liar, which is worse than a fake. I don't blame you if you don't want to be my friend anymore."

"Oh, *Emily,*" said Molly. "What you did was wrong, but friends don't stop being friends just because one of them makes a mistake! And anyway, it's my fault if I made it seem like I only liked you because you were good at the Flutophone. That's not true at all. I like you for a million reasons, but mostly I like you just because you're *you.* You're Emily. You're my *friend.*"

Emily looked at Molly and *almost* smiled a little.

Molly stood up. "Come on," she said to Emily. "Let's go back to the house. We need to come up with a plan, and it's too cold to talk in here."

"A plan?" asked Emily as she and Molly went down the stairs.

"Well, sure!" said Molly, "A plan for how Linda and Susan and I can help you do your solo on Saturday."

"You're going to help me?" asked Emily as they crossed the driveway.

"Well, sure!" said Molly again. "That's what friends are for!"

Now Emily really did smile a little, though it was too dark for Molly to see.

When the girls were back in bed, Emily put Grandy's dog tags under her pillow again. "Molly," she said earnestly, "thank you for being my friend. I like you very much, very much indeed. I never pretended about *that*."

"Oh," Molly teased gently, "you mean I'm not like oatmeal?"

"No!" said Emily.

"Maybe we can ask the Red Cross to send oatmeal to England, too," joked Molly, "along with all the smelly old turnips."

"And hot cross buns," added Emily.

Molly sat up in bed. "Emily!" she whispered excitedly. "That's it! I've thought of a way!"

"A way to what?" asked Emily.

"A way to help you do your solo," said Molly, "and a way that you can help England at the same time. But you're going to have to be very, very brave."

"Whatever it is, I'll do it," said Emily. *"Absolutely."*

★

The next morning, Molly and Emily presented Molly's plan to Linda and Susan, who liked it very much. Then all four girls stayed after school to talk to Miss Campbell.

"I'm very sorry that I lied about how much I practiced, Miss Campbell," Emily said sadly, after she had told the whole story.

"Well," said Miss Campbell, "I'm sorry, too. Promise me that starting now, you'll practice an extra thirty minutes every day for ten days so as to make the false numbers on your practice card true. Meanwhile, I can't think of any worse punishment than having to play your Flutophone in front of a crowd without having practiced enough. But the show is tomorrow evening. The programs have already been printed. So I'm afraid you'll have to play your 'America the Beautiful' solo, Emily."

"Yes, Miss Campbell," said Emily miserably.

"Miss Campbell," asked Molly, "is it okay if Linda and Susan and I are right behind Emily while she plays?"

Miss Campbell tilted her head. "You mean," she said, "give her a background so she can be camouflaged? Yes, I guess so."

"Thanks, Miss Campbell!" said the girls.

"Don't worry, Miss Campbell," said Molly. "We're going to be *great*."

★

Emily, Molly, Linda, and Susan worked very, very hard Friday afternoon, Friday evening, and all day Saturday until dinner. They practiced so much that by Saturday evening, when it was time for the show, Emily could play "America the Beautiful" without making *too* many mistakes. She was awfully glad, though, when the class gathered on the stage, that her friends Linda, Susan, and Molly were right behind her.

"Emily," Susan whispered, "Miss Campbell said you'd be camouflaged. But you look so pretty in that green dress Mrs. Gilford made for you that everyone's going to see you and love you."

Emily smiled bravely. "Thank you," she said.

The curtain went up and Miss Campbell announced the third grade. The whole class played "America the Beautiful" together first, and then Emily stepped forward.

With everyone in the whole auditorium

watching and listening, Emily played "America the Beautiful" all by herself on the Flutophone. But behind her, Molly, Linda, and Susan swirled and twirled using steps they knew from their tap dancing. Molly played the tambourine, Linda played the triangle, and Susan played the cymbals, crashing them nice and loud over the hard parts to hide Emily's mistakes. When the song was over, the audience clapped and cheered. Woody and Howie rushed forward and thumped Emily on the back, then waved their Flutophones in the air.

Now Emily did the bravest thing she had ever done in her life. She held up her hands for quiet. When everyone settled down, she said, "My name is Emily Bennett. I'm from England, and my parents are still there. My friends and I

would like to ask all of you to help England by donating canned food to the Red Cross. The Red Cross will send the food to England. Thank you."

Then Emily played her Flutophone while Molly, Linda, and Susan played their tambourine, triangle, and cymbals, tap danced, and sang:

When the song was over, the audience clapped and cheered.

America, America!
God shed His grace on thee!
So lend a hand
And send a can
Across the shining sea.

★

Afterward, everyone agreed that Emily's speech and the song about the cans was the best part of the whole show. But for Emily, the best part came after the show, when she and Molly, exhausted and exhilarated, were surrounded by people promising to bring cans to the Red Cross the very next day.

"My goodness," Emily overheard a lady say to Molly, "the little English girl spoke right up for England, didn't she?"

"Oh, yes," Emily heard Molly say. "My friend Emily is very brave."

45 × 10 = 450

467 Oak Street
Jefferson, Illinois, U.S.A.
Sunday, 16 April, 1944

Dear Mum and Dad,

How are you? I am fine.

For a long time, my friend Molly and I have been trying to find a way for me to help England. Please tell Grandy that finally, I can. (That's a pun, Dad.)

First, I had to be very, very brave! Here's what happened...

LOOKING BACK

CHILDREN OF WAR

The bombs that German planes dropped on London's factories and government buildings also destroyed people's homes, making life unsafe for all Londoners—even children.

As Molly told Emily, Emily's parents must have loved her very much to send her away. But war presents families with hard choices. More than anything else, loving parents like Emily's wanted their children to be safe. And London was *not* safe. Starting in 1940, German bombs fell on the city almost every night, in what became known as the *Blitz.* When air-raid sirens screamed warning of approaching German

planes, everyone had to scramble for the safety of backyard bomb shelters or take shelter in crowded *tube,* or subway, stations. People didn't know if their house or their neighbor's house would still be standing when

These Londoners slept in the tube, *or subway, to be safe from the bombs.*

70

MOTHERS
Send them out
of London

Give them a chance of greater safety and health

they emerged from a bomb shelter.

London was not healthy for children, either. In addition to the dangers caused by the bombs, there were shortages of food and clothing , and both were severely rationed. Houses were cold because there was little coal to heat with.

Everyone in England wanted English children to be safe and healthy, so the government created programs to help children *evacuate,* or move out of, London. Sometimes mothers and children moved to the countryside to live with family or friends. Sometimes kind strangers took mothers and children into their homes and

Carrying small suitcases and wearing tags showing their names and destinations, these children are shown leaving London.

shared what they had. But
many children were sent away
from London without their
parents. These children said sad farewells to their
parents, not knowing when they would see them again.
Like Emily, many were told to be "brave for England."

Other parents,
such as Emily's,
thought that even
the English country-
side wasn't safe
enough. They sent
their children over-
seas to Australia,

*English children being evacuated to
Australia, halfway around the world*

Canada, or the United States—countries far from the war. They believed that the dangerous journey by ship across submarine-infested ocean waters was less risky for their children than staying in England, where people feared an invasion by Germany.

The dangerous crossing of the Atlantic Ocean took about ten days, with ships traveling in *convoys,* or groups, for protection. In one crossing that carried children to Canada and the United States, 11 of the 28 ships in the convoy were sunk—although none of *those* ships carried children. In all, about 14,000 children were evacuated from Britain. But when one of the evacuation ships was sunk and 77 children lost their lives, the government abandoned its overseas evacuation program.

By the time Emily was sent to America in 1944, only individual

Notes of congratulations sent to an English evacuee, Shiela McKay, in 1940. The ship she was taking to Canada was torpedoed, but the children bravely survived in lifeboats.

Children evacuated from London enjoy tea in the garden of their host's home.

families sent their children overseas. Some evacuees had good experiences and formed lifelong friendships. Other children had a harder time of it and were treated more as helping hands than as guests to protect.

The long separations were hard on families, of course, and when families were far apart, letters like Emily's to her parents were very important. One seven-year-old boy, returning to England from Canada at the end of the war, hadn't seen his parents since he was three. He had to be introduced to them anew, and then he asked, "But how do I know that she is my mother?"

Posters encouraged women to assist with the government's evacuation efforts.

Evacuees eagerly read a letter from home.

Jewish children arriving in England in 1939

British children were not the only ones to be *displaced*, or moved about, because of the war. People concerned about children's safety created a rescue effort for thousands of refugee children in Europe. The *Kindertransport,* or children's transport, program brought close to 10,000 children from Germany, Austria, Czechoslovakia, and Poland to Britain. Most were Jewish children who had lost their parents because of Nazi Germany's violence toward Jews. Reaching safety in England, they were the lucky ones—the Kindertransport program did not last long enough to save most of Europe's Jewish children, and more than one million Jewish children lost their lives.

Although World War Two was not fought on American soil, American children were affected, too. Almost every family had a son, brother, or father away at war and most families had someone doing war work on the home front.

Some of the American children most affected by the war were Japanese American. After planes from Japan bombed Pearl Harbor

An American soldier says good-bye to his family as he heads off to war.

in Hawaii, some Americans were afraid that Japanese Americans would have greater loyalty to the land of their ancestors than to America. So the American

Japanese Americans were forced to leave their homes and live in remote internment camps.

government made Japanese American families give up their homes and jobs and move into *internment camps* located in remote desert areas. In the camps, children attended school and families could stay together, but barbed wire fences and armed guards prevented them from leaving until the war ended in 1945. The president's wife, Eleanor Roosevelt, was one of many

One of the ways that children coped with life in the camps was by playing baseball.

First Lady Eleanor Roosevelt visiting an internment camp

Americans who spoke out against this unfair treatment of American citizens. And Japanese Americans fought hard to prove that they were loyal Americans. In the end, almost none were found to have been traitors or spies. One *regiment,* or group, of Japanese American soldiers fighting in Europe won the most medals for bravery of any American regiment.

World War Two changed the lives of people everywhere. Even very young children had to learn to be as brave as soldiers. When the war ended at last, and families were reunited, it sometimes took a while for them to get to know one another again. But of all the changes the war brought, children readjusting to normal, safe lives at home in peacetime was surely the most welcome change of all.

At war's end, these British families are finally reunited.

A SNEAK PEEK AT

MEET
Molly

Dad's away, Mom's working, and there are turnips for dinner. It seems to Molly that everything is different because of the war—and she's not sure she likes all the changes.

olly had smelled trouble as soon as she walked into the kitchen. It was a heavy, hot smell, kind of like the smell of dirty socks. She saw an orange heap on her plate. She made up her mind right away not to eat it. "What's this orange stuff?" she asked.

Mrs. Gilford glared at her. "Polite children do not refer to food as *stuff*," said Mrs. Gilford. "The vegetable which you are lucky enough to have on your plate is mashed turnip."

"I like turnips," said Ricky, and he shoveled a forkful into his mouth.

That rat Ricky, thought Molly. She looked over at her older sister Jill. Jill was putting ladylike bites of turnip in her mouth and washing them down with long, quiet sips of water. Almost all of the horrible orange stuff was gone from her plate.

Molly sighed. In the old days, before Jill turned fourteen and got stuck-up, Molly used to be able to count on her to make a fuss about things like turnips. But lately, Molly had to do it all herself. This new grown-up Jill was a terrible disappointment to Molly. If that's what happened to you when you got to be fourteen, Molly would rather be nine forever.

The turnips sat on Molly's plate getting cold. With her fork, Molly carefully pushed her meat and potatoes to a corner of her plate so that not a speck of turnip would touch them and ruin them. "Disgusting," she said softly.

"There will be no such language at this table," said Mrs. Gilford. "And anyone who fails to finish her turnips will have no dessert. Nor will she be allowed to leave the table until the turnips are gone."

That's why Molly was still at the kitchen table facing a plate of cold turnips at 8:46 P.M. *None of this would have happened if Dad were home*, she thought.

Molly's father was a doctor. When American soldiers started fighting in World War Two, Dr. McIntire joined the Army. He had been gone for seven months. Molly missed him every single minute of every single day.

Now it was almost nine o'clock. It was getting cold in the kitchen. Molly was lonely. She looked at the turnips, then put a tiny forkful in her mouth. Just then Ricky burst through the swinging kitchen door.

"How do you like eating old, cold, moldy brains?" he teased. Then he ran out.

"Ricky, you rat!" Molly said. "I'm going to get you!" She started to get up from the chair.

From behind the door Ricky chanted, "Nyah, nyah, nyah-nyah nyah! You can't leave the table!"

"Ricky, stop it!" yelled Molly. But Ricky was right. The turnips were still on her plate and she was stuck. To make matters worse, Molly heard her mother calling good-bye to the car pool she rode with from Red Cross headquarters.

Now Mom will be mad at me, too, thought Molly. *Now she'll never make my Halloween costume. Now everyone in the house will be mad at me for making*

Mom upset. And all because of these terrible turnips.

Mrs. McIntire walked in the back door, looked at Molly, looked at the plate, and knew immediately what had happened. "Well, Molly," she said. "I see we had turnips from the Victory garden tonight."

"Mom," said Molly, "I hate turnips. And Mrs. Gilford says I can't leave the table until I eat them. I'll be here until I die, because I will never eat these."

"I see," said Molly's mother. "Do you mind if I join you for a while? Not until you die, of course— just while I have a cup of tea. And while I'm at the stove, why don't I reheat those turnips for you?"

"It won't help," said Molly.

But Mrs. McIntire scooped up the turnips and put them in a frying pan. "I think we can spare a bit of our sugar and butter rations to add to the turnips," she said, almost to herself. "And a little cinnamon, too."

Soon a delicious aroma filled the kitchen. Mrs. McIntire spooned the turnips back onto Molly's plate.

Molly took a deep breath, raised a small forkful to her lips, and tasted it. It wasn't so bad. In fact, it was pretty good—not at all like old, cold, moldy brains. She ate another forkful.

Mrs. McIntire sat down with her tea. "When I was about your age," she said, "my mother made sardines on toast for dinner one night. Little dead fish on toast! She said I could not leave the table until the sardines were gone. So when she wasn't looking I put them into my napkin. Then I stuck my napkin into my pocket.

"Later that night I was playing checkers with my father. Our cat Bessy yowled and meowed and climbed all over me. Finally, she pulled the napkin out of my pocket. The sardines spilled out all over the rug."

"Oh, Mom!" laughed Molly.

"Oh, Molly," sighed Mrs. McIntire. "Sometimes we have to do things whether we like it or not." She reached across the table and brushed Molly's bangs out of her eyes. "I know this war is hard on you. And I know you miss your father. I miss him, too."

"Everything is so different with Dad gone," said Molly. "Nothing is the way it used to be anymore."

"The war *has* changed things," said Mrs. McIntire. "But some things are still the same. Isn't Ricky still Ricky? And you are still my olly Molly. And I am still me." She gave Molly's hand a squeeze.

*"The war **has** changed things," said Mrs. McIntire.
"But some things are still the same."*

READ ALL OF MOLLY'S STORIES,
available at bookstores and *americangirl.com.*

MEET MOLLY • An American Girl
While her father is fighting in World War Two,
Molly and her brother start their own war at home.

MOLLY LEARNS A LESSON • A School Story
Molly and her friends plan a secret project to help the
war effort, and learn about allies and cooperation.

MOLLY'S SURPRISE • A Christmas Story
Molly makes plans for Christmas surprises,
but she ends up being surprised herself.

HAPPY BIRTHDAY, MOLLY! • A Springtime Story
An English girl comes to stay with Molly,
but she's not what Molly expects!

MOLLY SAVES THE DAY • A Summer Story
At summer camp, Molly has to pretend to be her
friend's enemy and face her own fears, too.

CHANGES FOR MOLLY • A Winter Story
Dad will return from the war any day! Will he arrive in time
to see the "grown-up" Molly perform as Miss Victory?

◆

WELCOME TO MOLLY'S WORLD • 1944
American history is lavishly illustrated
with photographs, illustrations, and
excerpts from real girls' letters and diaries.